C.L.O.N.C.
STRIKES BACK

PUFFIN BOOKS

Published by the Penguin Group
Penguin Books Ltd, 80 Strand, London WC2R 0RL, England
Penguin Group (USA) Inc., 375 Hudson Street, New York, New York 10014,
USA Penguin Group (Canada), 90 Eglinton Avenue East, Suite 700,
Toronto, Ontario, Canada M4P 2Y3 (a division of Pearson Penguin Canada Inc.)
Penguin Ireland, 25 St Stephen's Green, Dublin 2, Ireland
a division of Penguin Books Ltd)
Penguin Group (Australia), 707 Collins Street, Melbourne, Victoria 3008,
Australia (a division of Pearson Australia Group Pty Ltd)
Penguin Books India Pvt Ltd, 11 Community Centre, Panchsheel Park,
New Delhi – 110 017, India
Penguin Group (NZ), 67 Apollo Drive, Rosedale, Auckland 0632,
New Zealand (a division of Pearson New Zealand Ltd)
Penguin Books (South Africa) (Pty) Ltd, Block D, Rosebank Office Park,
181 Jan Smuts Avenue, Parktown North, Gauteng 2193, South Africa

Penguin Books Ltd, Registered Offices: 80 Strand, London WC2R 0RL, England

puffinbooks.com

First published 2013
001

Written by Sue Behrent
Illustrations by Abigail Ryder

Text and illustrations copyright © Mind Candy Ltd, 2013
Moshi Monsters is a trademark of Mind Candy Ltd. All rights reserved

The moral right of the author and illustrator has been asserted

Set in Adobe Garamond Pro
Printed in Great Britain by Clays Ltd, St Ives plc

British Library Cataloguing in Publication Data
A CIP catalogue record for this book is available from the British Library

ISBN: 978-1-409-39222-4

MIX
Paper from
responsible sources
FSC
www.fsc.org   FSC® C018179

ALWAYS LEARNING   **PEARSON**

C.L.O.n.C.
STRIKES BACK

T SHREWMAN

PUFFIN

CONTENTS

Chapter 1

SANDY DRAIN SHENNANIGANS

Deep in the jungle on Music Island, aboard a crash-landed spaceship, Captain Squirk looked up from the scans he'd been studying and frowned thoughtfully at the Super Moshis.

'I've got some good news . . . and some bad news,' said the tiny Zoshling. 'The good news is the *Rhapsody 2*'s ZPS has located one of my missing crew members. If you can rescue my friend, that only leaves two more Zoshlings to find! Then the *Rhapsody 2* can take off again and investigate this new star in the Grosshead Nebula system.'

'Where does the ZPS say this Zoshling is?' asked Katsuma excitedly, ignoring the bit about the star.

'Somewhere called the Sandy Drain Hotel,' said Squirk, scratching his head.

The Super Moshis exchanged astonished looks. What would a Zoshling from the planet Symphonia be doing at the celebrity hotspot on Music Island? Wow. They were going to do some serious star-spotting!

'Don't forget the bad news,' Squirk reminded them, waggling his finger. The Super Moshis' grins vanished. 'That new star I told you about? It's getting bigger.'

'Bigger? How is that possible?' asked Luvli, her fluttery eyes widening.

'I don't know.' Squirk shook his head. 'Worse, super-scientist Tamara Tesla called to say it seems to be melting the snow on Mount Sillimanjaro. Melted snow means the sea levels are rising . . . and Monstro City is in danger of drowning!'

The Super Moshis gasped in unison.

'Super Moshis,' pleaded Captain Squirk, 'you must

return all my Zoshling crew as soon as possible so we can lift off and solve this interstellar puzzle – before it's too late!'

'We'll leave for the Sandy Drain Hotel at once, Captain,' said Poppet gravely. 'You can count on us.'

'Stop it, Furi,' hissed Diavlo out of the corner of his mouth. 'What are you doing digging about in those pot plants?'

Furi stumbled away from the little garden outside

the reception of the famous Sandy Drain Hotel. 'I'm feeling peckish,' he replied. 'I was just looking for some grubs.' 'Well, don't,' scolded Diavlo. 'It's embarrassing.

This is an eight-star hotel, not the Gombala Gombala Jungle! We have to act cool. We have to act with decorum. We have to –'

'Hey, Furi! Check this out!' Zommer yelled as he whizzed round and round inside a huge brass revolving door.

'That. Is. AWESOME!' Furi squealed, rushing towards the grand entrance to join in the fun.

'Gah!' said Diavlo, slapping his forehead. 'I give up!'

Diavlo, Poppet, Katsuma and Luvli ushered Furi and Zommer through the door and into the swanky lobby. The Moshis gaped at the groovy purple walls and funky furniture.

'Wow!' Poppet exclaimed. 'This is so cool!'

'Isn't it? It's going to be full of celebrities,' Luvli sighed as she spied Taylor Miffed relaxing on a sofa in the corner.

'OK, OK. Don't lose it!' Katsuma warned. 'Remember, we're here on a mission. We have to find this Zoshling and return it to the *Rhapsody 2* – and quickly. So let me handle this.'

He set off across the plush lilac carpet towards the reception desk. He'd only taken half a dozen steps when someone grabbed his arm.

'What are you lot doing here?' Simon Growl snapped. 'I hope you aren't going to cause any more trouble.'

'Trouble?' Katsuma frowned. 'Oh, if you're talking about that hot little incident on your Sneerjet –'

Simon Growl's hair growled.

'Well, we've already apologized for that. It's not like we cause havoc everywhere we go.'

The words were barely out of Katsuma's mouth before he heard an almighty crash behind him. The crowded hotel lobby fell silent. Turning slowly, he saw Furi and Zommer sprawled on the floor, cackling gleefully. They'd flown out of the revolving door, hit several pot plants mid-air and crashed to the ground. Wet soil was scattered across the pristine purple carpet.

'You were saying, Katsuma?' Growl snickered. His hair chortled too.

Katsuma stared at the mess, speechless.

'Are these . . . creatures . . . friends of yooooooours, Mr Growl?' boomed an annoyed voice.

Katsuma turned away from his embarrassing friends to find a large, smartly dressed cow looming over him. Her jaw flapped uncontrollably.

7

'Nope,' he replied. 'I'll be sunbathing if anyone needs me, Frau BrownKau. *Ciao*!' And with that he scarpered off to the pool.

Frau Now BrownKau, the manager of the Sandy Drain Hotel, focused her withering gaze on Katsuma.

'Can I help yooooou with anything?' she drawled haughtily, her teeth chomping. Pain creased her features every time she spoke.

'Er, yes. We'd like a room, please,' Katsuma said nervously. The rest of the Super Moshis gathered around behind him. 'For all of us.'

'That will beeeeeeee five million Rox . . . per night,' Frau Now BrownKau winced.

'What? Are you kidding?' Diavlo gasped. 'No one could afford that!'

'Our prices ensure we keeeeeeep the riff-raff out,' snapped BrownKau, looking the Super Moshis up and down, her jaw jerking wildly in all directions.

'Dude, are you all right? Have you eaten something funny?' Zommer asked. 'I can't help but notice your gnashers working overtime in there.'

'My teeeeeth don't fit prooooooperly,' she grunted, her eyes rolling in agony.

The Super Moshis grimaced.

'I'll tell yooooou what,' Frau BrownKau said suddenly. 'I'll let you stay for freeeeee – if you locate my false teeeeeth.'

'You're on,' agreed Poppet quickly before the moody cow could change her mind. 'Come on, Super Moshis, let's play 'find the false teeth'!'

The Super Moshis left the cool, shaded hotel lobby and stepped into the bright, sunny pool area.

The sparkling pool was huge. Its perimeter was dotted with big spa rooms where the gooperstar guests received their treatments.

'This certainly beats swimming at DJ Quack's A-Quack-tic Centre on Taki Taki Island,' said Luvli as she surveyed the celebrities relaxing on their sun loungers. 'Hmph! I see Simon Growl's here.'

'Oh, and there's Zack Binspin!' Poppet squealed. 'Let go over and say hi.'

'First things first, Poppet,' said Katsuma. 'We've got to find Frau Now BrownKau's teeth.'

'First things first nothing! I'm starving! I've got to have something to eat and drink!' Furi cried, his stomach grumbling loudly as he snatched up the hotel menu from a nearby table.

'We can't possibly afford the prices at the Sandy Drain Hotel,' said Poppet, looking over Furi's shoulder at the menu. 'Crispy Bat Wings, 120 Rox! Bongo Colada, 78 Rox! It's daylight robbery!'

'It's celebrity snobbery, that's what it is!' Zommer said, outraged. 'But at least the water's free. Here, Furi, wrap your furry gob round this,' he added, handing Furi a half-drunk glass someone had left beside a sun lounger.

'Cheers, Zom,' said Furi. He was about to take a sip when he spotted something at the bottom of the glass. 'Arrrrgh! Wassat?'

The Super Moshis bashed heads as they all tried to take a look.

'It's Frau Now BrownKau's missing teeth!' laughed Diavlo, fishing them out.

'I must have left them by the pooooool when I went to give a treatment in one of the spa rooooooooms,' said

Frau BrownKau as she snatched her false teeth from Furi's grubby hand.

Frau BrownKau spat the problem choppers on to the carpet, popped in her own and strode out to the pool area without another word.

The Moshis all looked at the discarded teeth.

Suddenly, they sprouted legs and began dashing about madly, gnashing and chattering away!

'Oh my, it's a Jabbering Jibberling!' Luvli exclaimed. 'The poor thing's been stuck in that old cow's mouth the whole time!'

'How cruel!' said Poppet, and bent over to speak to the little Moshling. 'Are you OK?'

'Ewwww-it-smelled-like-rotting-wet-grass-in-there-but-I'm-OK-thanks-to-you!!' the Jabbering Jibberling chittered. 'My-name's-Rofl!-What's-yours?'

Poppet opened her mouth to answer but Rofl chattered on.

'I'd-get-out-of-here-if-I-was-you. Don't-trust-Frau-BrownKau! She-does-strange-things.'

'We can't. We're on a mission,' explained Diavlo. 'In fact, we're looking for a Zoshling — have you seen one around here?'

'A-what-ling?' Rofl asked, hopping from foot to foot. 'I-don't-know-what-that-is-but-I-can-tell-you-that-Frau-BrownKau-keeps-a-strange-pet-in-Spa-Room-Three!'

Chapter 2

ZACK BINSPIN HELPS OUT

'What exactly do we suspect Frau Now BrownKau of doing exactly?' Katsuma asked as the Supers gather around the door of Spa Room 3.

'She held a Jabbering Jibberling captive in her mouth, Katsuma!' Luvli cried. 'I suspect she's a very bad old cow!'

'Same here,' said Poppet. 'Anyway, it won't hurt to check out this strange pet Rofl told us about.'

Diavlo, Zommer and Furi all nodded in agreement.

'Okay,' said Katsuma, with a shrug. Checking to see

that nobody was looking, he reached over and turned the doorknob. 'It's locked.'

'Put your back into it, dude,' said Zommer, pushing Katsuma out of the way.

He gave the door a terrific shove with his shoulder. It didn't budge.

'I'm the strongest here,' Furi said, brushing him aside. 'Let me have a go.'

'Strong? Wrong! This needs the subtle arts of my Sparkle Shower,' Luvli said, grabbing at the doorknob.

'Out of the way!' Zommer cried, slapping her hand.

'You don't know what you're doing!' Katsuma shouted, pushing him back again.

The Super Moshis were so busy bickering amongst themselves that they didn't notice a shadow looming up behind them.

'What's going on here?'

The Supers spun round guiltily.

'Zack Binspin!' Poppet cried.

They were all relieved to see it was the pint-sized gooperstar and not Frau Now BrownKau!

'Hey, Super Moshis! I didn't think I'd see you guys again so soon,' cooed Zack. 'What are you doing here?'

'We're searching for a missing Zoshling,' explained Furi. 'It's hidden somewhere at the Sandy Drain Hotel.'

'A Zoshling? I thought that was an Undercover YapYap snack!' Zack giggled. 'Anyway, I'm glad to see you. I didn't get to thank you properly after you saved me from being mobbed at Simon Growl's scareport.'

'Hey, no sweat, Zack,' smiled Katsuma.

'There was plenty of sweat, believe me!' Zack giggled. 'To pay you back, I'd love to give you a signed photo . . .'

'That'd be great!' Poppet said.

'Coooool! I've got some spare pics in my bag.'

Zack led the way over to his poolside sun lounger and began rummaging in his bag. He pulled out a stack of photos and signed one with a flourish:

'Thank you, Zack. I'll cherish it always,' sighed Poppet, hugging the photo to her chest. The rest of the Supers rolled their eyes.

'Of course you will, baby,' Zack winked.

'Mr Binspin!' a voice barked.

The Supers looked up to see Frau Now BrownKau striding towards them.

'It's time for your treatment! Go to Spa Room One,' she ordered.

'I don't have my key card, baby. I left it in my safety deposit box at reception,' Zack explained as she grabbed him by the shoulder and marched him towards the spa room.

'I'll let you in,' she barked as she unlocked the door and pushed Zack inside. 'But next time –'

The Super Moshis couldn't hear the rest as Frau Now BrownKau firmly closed the door to Spa Room 1 behind her.

'Phew! That was close,' said Luvli. 'If Der Frau had caught us trying to break into Spa Room Three . . . '

Luvli gulped at the thought of what the scary cow might do to them.

'C'mon, Supers,' said Katsuma. 'While Frau Now BrownKau is busy with Zack's treatment, let's see if we can get the key card for Spa Room Three from reception.'

'Good idea!' Poppet's eyes narrowed in determination. 'We have to get to the bottom of this mystery pet situation.'

The Super Moshis found Rofl in charge of reception in Frau Now BrownKau's absence.

'Can we get the key card to Spa Room Three please, Rofl?' Luvli asked, batting her lashes appealingly. 'We're curious to see the Frau's strange pet you told us about.'

'I'd-love-to-help-you,' chittered Rofl as he darted about tidying up the reception area. 'But-Frau-BrownKau-keeps-all-the-key-cards-on-a-chain-she-wears-on-her-belt.'

The Moshis frowned. What now?

'Oh!' Poppet suddenly exclaimed. 'We heard Zack Binspin tell Frau Now BrownKau that he'd left his key card to Spa Room One in his safety deposit box,' said Poppet. 'It's not the right room, but maybe we could borrow it and start there . . .?'

'Well-she-sometimes-lets-special-guests-keep-their-key-cards-in-their-personal-safety-deposit-boxes,' said Rofl, gesturing to the wall of safes behind him. 'But-you'll-need-Mr-Binspin's-code-to-get-inside-his-safe.'

'No worries, we've got Zack's code,' Katsuma piped up.

'We do?' Furi scratched his head. 'How? When?'

'Exhibit A,' said Katsuma smugly. 'Zack's autographed photo please, Poppet.'

He held out his paw and Poppet reluctantly handed him Zack's photo.

Katsuma pointed to the number Zack had scrawled under his signature.

'This 301 Zack's written here? It's probably his room number,' he explained. 'Am I right, Rofl?'

'It-is. I-just-cleaned-his-suite-this-morning,' nodded Rofl. 'Like-a-lot-of-our-music-celebrity-guests-Mr-Binspin-likes-to-trash-his-room-every-night!'

'I thought Zack was from Brashcan Alley not Trashcan Alley?' Zommer muttered to Furi as he elbowed him in his furry ribs. 'Get it? Trashcan . . .

and he likes to trash his room . . . get it? Eh?'

'Yeah, I got it all right, Zom,' said Furi, rolling his eyes. 'I only wish I hadn't! It would've been much funnier if you'd said –'

'So it seems to me that Zack isn't exactly a brainiac,' said Katsuma, talking over Furi. 'He's the sort of Moshling who wouldn't have room in his bonce for anything other than sucking up to Simon Growl, combing his luscious locks, lazing beside the pool and coo-cooing like a –'

Katsuma suddenly caught Poppet's eye. Her face was turning redder and redder with every Binspin insult!

'Anyway . . . ahem . . . let's just say I don't think he'd bother thinking up a code for his safety deposit box if he could just use his room number,' he finished hurriedly.

'Let's stop wasting time and try it already!' Diavlo huffed. He flew over to the wall of safety deposit boxes and began turning the combination dial of Zack's box. 'Three . . .' *click, click* '. . . zero . . .' *click, click* '. . . one . . . ' **CLUNK!**

The locking mechanism drew back and the door opened to reveal the key card for Spa Room 1.

'We have entry!' Diavlo laughed as he grabbed the key card.

Luvli stepped back from where she'd pressed her ear to the door of Spa Room 1 and turned to the Supers gathered behind her.

'Frau Now BrownKau's definitely not in there,' she said decisively. 'I can hear some muffled conversation, but it sounds like Zack is singing to himself or something.'

The Super Moshis nodded and Luvli swiped the key card to unlock the door.

It swung partly open and the Supers could hear weird muffled speech.

'*Mmmmph! Mmmmm-mm, mmmMPH!*'

'What's that?' Zommer asked as he pushed the door wide open.

'Twinkly-Dinkers! What's going on here?' Poppet exclaimed.

In a large chair in the middle of the room sat Zack Binspin. But he was barely visible under a fast-growing mop of hair! Long tresses bound his arms and legs to the chair. His flourishing fringe flowed down from his head and over his face. He couldn't move, he couldn't

see, he couldn't hear and he could barely breathe!

'*Mmmmmmmmmmph! MMMMMMPH!*' Zack's muffled pleas fought their way through his locks and he thrashed about in the chair.

'Quick, grab those clippers!' Luvli yelled, pointing to the nearby dressing table.

Diavlo snatched them up hurriedly and flipped the switch, but the clippers just emitted a mangled buzzing sound and the blades wouldn't work at all!

'Drat! They're as useless as a Froggie Doggie at a swimming carnival!' he cried.

'Guys, we have to do something now!' Zommer shrieked. 'Zack can't breathe!'

Log in to **MOSHIMONSTERS.COM**, click the **ENTER SECRET CODE** button and type the **last word** on the **thirteenth line** on **page 88**. Your surprise free gift will appear in your treasure chest!

Chapter 3

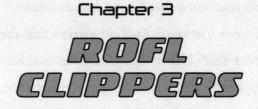

ROFL CLIPPERS

'Everybody shush! I'm trying to think!' Katsuma ordered. The Super Moshis fell silent as Katsuma began muttering rapidly under his breath. 'OK. We need to cut Zack's hair super-quickly. We've got to get those broken clippers working crazy fast. Which means we need to find something crazy and something fast. Which means we need . . .'

Katsuma looked up suddenly.

'Luvli, go get Rofl!'

Luvli flew straight out of the door in search of the manic Moshling. Meanwhile, the remaining Super

Moshis continued wrestling with Zack's locks.

'Once we've saved Zack we need to find the swine who did this!' Diavlo frowned as he yanked back a swathe of hair that was snaking round Zack's neck.

'*MmmmmMMMMPH!*' Zack squealed as he squirmed in his chair.

'I don't think it's swine we're after, Diavlo,' said Poppet. 'I think it's cow . . .'

Suddenly, Luvli burst through the door, dragging Rofl behind her.

'Here's Rofl, Katsuma! What do you want him to do?' Luvli panted.

'Take these, Rofl!' Katsuma called as he threw him the broken clippers. 'And work those choppers of yours!'

Rofl leaped up and caught them in mid-air, deftly replacing the broken blades with his own snappy teeth to make all-new Rofl clippers! Then he launched himself at Zack and began to gnash at the growing hair.

First, Rofl chewed through the hair that tied Zack's hands and feet to the chair. Next, he bit through the plait that had wound round his neck.

Then Rofl freed Zack's mouth and nose, and, lastly, he uncovered the Moshling's big brown eyes!

Rofl jumped to the floor, disentangled himself from the clippers and looked up at Zack, whose moptop was back to its normal shape and size! The Super Moshis burst into applause.

'I guess you could say Rofl is Zack's Gnashcan Ally!' Furi snickered to Zommer. 'And that is how you tell a punny joke, Zom!'

Poppet shushed her friends and looked expectantly at Zack, who was yet to speak. The gooperstar frowned, spat out a furball and smiled.

'Gee, thanks, everyone!' he whispered as he rubbed his throat gingerly. 'I thought my beautiful locks were going to be the death of me.'

'Well, your fringe in particular is dead gorgeous,' laughed Zommer. Poppet elbowed him grumpily.

'Can you tell us what happened, Zack?' Katsuma asked.

'It was Frau Now BrownKau,' Zack replied. 'She said she had a new killer treatment for my hair. I didn't

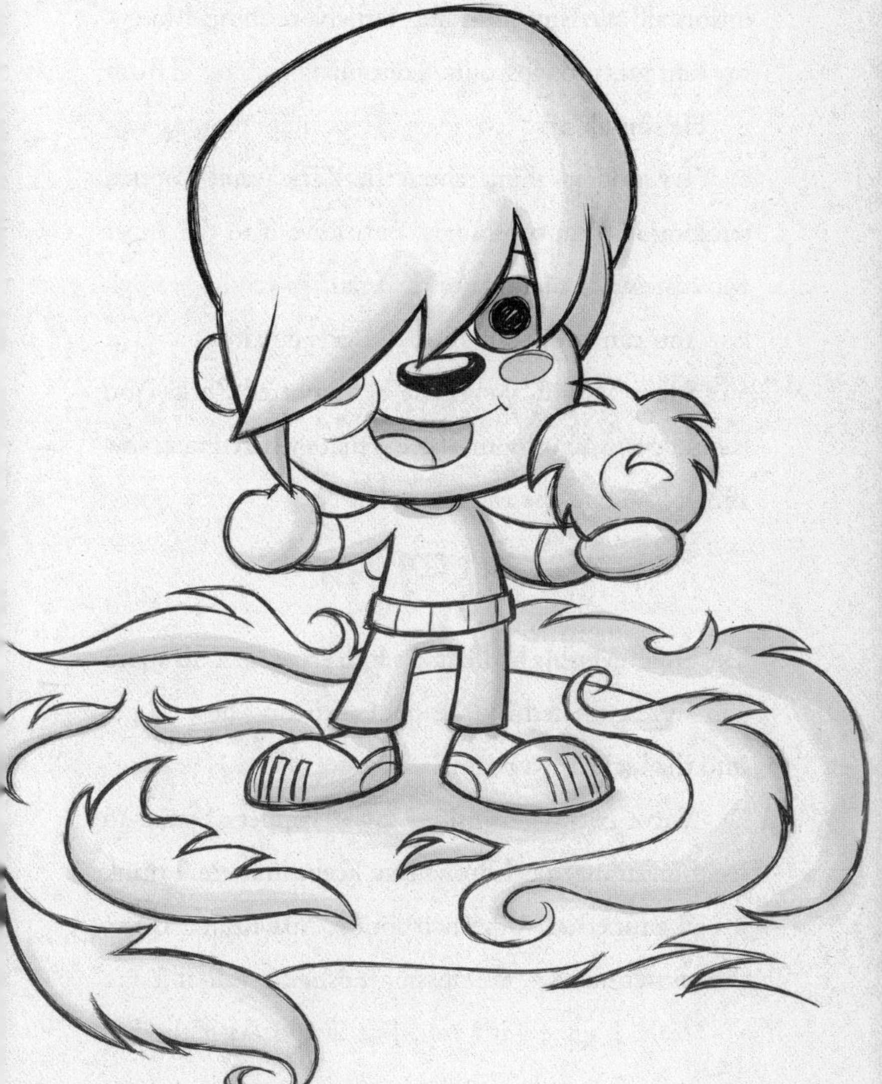

know she meant it literally! She emptied a bottle of lotion all over my head and left. Next thing I knew, my hair was growing outta control!'

He shuddered.

'Try not to think about it, Zack,' said Poppet, stroking his arm soothingly. 'Just leave it to the Super Moshis. We'll take care of the Frau.'

'You-can-count-me-in-too!' Rofl added.

'Super Moshis, you're the best,' purred Zack. 'You should go to Spa Room Three – that's where Frau Now BrownKau said she was headed . . .'

The Super Moshis had left Zack to recover in his room and were gathered by the pool, debating how to get into the locked spa room.

'We've got to get inside,' urged Poppet. 'I want to see this "strange pet" BrownKau keeps in there. I think it's all connected – the hair lotion, Spa Room Three, the mysterious pet, the missing Zoshling – all of it!'

'Yeah, I agree with you. But it's not as if the key

card is just going to fall into our laps now, is it?' Luvli said, frowning.

'Fall into our laps? No. Fall to the bottom of the pool? Maybe,' Furi said, peering into the watery depths of the swimming pool.

'What are you talking about, Furi?' Zommer asked, joining his friend at the edge of the water.

'There, can you see it?' Furi said, pointing. 'On the bottom of the pool. It looks like a key card. Dunno if it's the one we're looking for, but let's fish it out and see.'

'Great idea, dude,' smiled Zommer. 'In you go and get it.'

'Who do you think I am, Diavlo?' Furi huffed. 'This isn't Loch Mess and I'm no Ginger McMoshling – OCH AYE!'

'I wish Octo was here,' said Zommer. 'She'd fish the key card out for us.'

'That reminds me of something,' said Poppet slowly. 'Say that last bit again, Zom.'

'I said Octo would fish it out for us,' Zommer repeated.

'Fish – that's it! I saw a fish hanging on the wall in Spa Room One. It had a hook in its mouth!' Poppet cried. 'I'll run and get it – you get hold of a long stick!'

Poppet ran to fetch the hook and Katsuma turned to Rofl.

'I don't know what she's planning, but can you get hold of a long stick?' he asked the Jabbering Jibberling.

'I-know-just-the-thing!' Rofl said, racing back into the hotel.

Moments later, Poppet returned with a slippery hook and Rofl reappeared with a broken tiki torch clamped between his teeth.

'What are you going to do, Poppet?' Furi asked.

'It's time to get "reel", Super Moshis!' she giggled in reply, and tied the hook to the torch to make a fishing rod.

She plunged it into the pool and raked the hook along the bottom.

Sure enough, the rod snagged the key card and Poppet brought it up to the surface truimphantly.

'Excellent; it is for Spa Room Three!' Luvli said,

clapping Poppet on the back. 'How did you come up with that? It was amazing!'

'I don't know, really,' said Poppet, suddenly blushing shyly.

The Super Moshis hurried over to Spa Room 3. Zommer nudged Furi.

'What d'you think we're gonna find in there?' he whispered, bewildered.

'Whatever it is . . . it won't be good,' said Furi.

The door to Spa Room 3 creaked open and the Super Moshis stepped inside. A rickety flight of stairs descended underground in front of them and they could hear the sound of machinery churning below their feet.

'Not exactly five-star facilities,' muttered Diavlo as he gazed at the greasy green gloop splattered on the floor and stairs. 'I wonder what that green stuff is . . .'

'Don't touch it,' said Poppet quickly. 'I bet it's the same stuff Frau Now BrownKau used on Zack's hair.'

The Super Moshis stepped carefully around the goop and crept down the stairs.

'Holy Hickopotamus!' Luvli exclaimed. They'd walked into an enormous underground cellar. The oily smell of cogs and cranks filled the air. A huge conveyor belt rolled along, carrying bottles of the green gloop, and mechanical arms were packing them into boxes. The Moshis could barely hear themselves think over the hiss, thump and whirr of the moving parts.

'Look, there's something stuck above the conveyor belt!' Poppet shouted. 'It's being squeezed like a lemon!'

The Super Moshis peered into the murky half-light and could just make out two pistons crushing a small purple creature.

'I think we've found our missing Zoshling, guys,' Diavlo cried.

'It looks like Der Frau is squeezing the goop out of this little guy,' Poppet replied. 'And it's obviously powerful stuff if she's bottling it!'

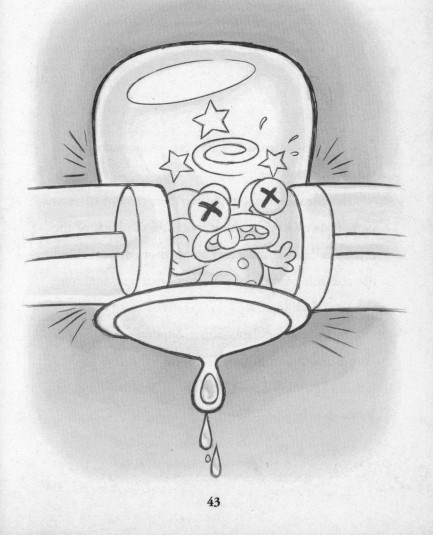

Chapter 4

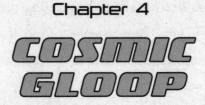

COSMIC GLOOP

'Moo-hahahaha! What are yoooooooooooooou doing here?'

The Moshis froze at the terrifying sound of Frau Now BrownKau's shrieking voice. At the back of the murky cellar, the mad cow stepped out from behind the controls of the giant machine that was squishing the poor Zoshling.

'You're tooooo late, Super Moshis!' she mooed. 'You're not going to stop me now!' The cow lifted a hose and pointed it straight at them, her hoof hovering over a switch.

'The green gloop! She's going to blast us with it!' shouted Katsuma.

SPLUT!

A gob of green gloop splashed at his feet.

'Quick!' said Poppet. 'Get behind here!'

The Super Moshis cowered behind a stack of crates as huge splodges of green gloop flew through the air towards them and splattered just a few metres away.

SPLUT! SPLUT! SPLUT!

'Looks like we're stuck here,' Diavlo whispered, hugging a frightened Rofl to him. 'We won't be able to get close enough to the Frau to sabotage her gloop gun and rescue that poor Zoshling.'

'Don't-worry-Super-Moshis-I've-got-this-one,' said Rofl suddenly, and before they could say anything the courageous Jabbering Jibberling tottered out from behind the crates, right into the line of fire! He bravely jittered towards Frau Now BrownKau, dodging behind boxes and trolleys, narrowly missing being splurged by the hose with every step.

Frau Now BrownKau looked more and more angry as she wrestled with the hose, trying to blast the tiny Moshling as he tottered ever closer.

'Where's he going? What's the little guy's plan?' said Furi.

'I don't know, but let's distract her!' said Zommer.

The Super Moshis started shouting and waving their arms to attract Frau BrownKau's attention and she angrily directed her blasts away from Rofl and towards them – giving Rofl enough time to creep up behind her and . . . give her a good bite of revenge right where it hurts! He clamped his choppers on her bovine backside and didn't let go.

"**Arrrrrrrgggggggghhhhh!**" screamed BrownKau. Her face creased in agony and she dropped the hose.

Rofl opened his teeth and dropped to the floor, just as the horrible cow tapped her wrist and vanished into thin air – taking the bottled gloop with her!

'You-can-come-out-now! Frau-BrownKau-has-gone!' Rofl chattered. One by one spikes, ears, fuzzy mops and star-tipped stems rose slowly from behind the packing crates.

'What do you mean "gone"?' Diavlo asked, scratching his head. 'Where did she go?'

'I-don't-know. She-fiddled-with-a-small-device-on-her-wrist-and-disappeared-before-my-eyes,' Rofl explained. 'And-she-took-her-bottled-gunk- with-her-too.'

'My cosmic gloop . . .' a small voice whispered. 'Very dangerous . . .'

The Super Moshis jumped. The poor Zoshling was still stuck inside BrownKau's infernal machine! Poppet quickly unclamped him from between the pistons and set him down on the floor.

'We need to get this little guy back to the *Rhapsody 2* now,' Katsuma said.

'Are you sure there's not enough time to say goodbye to Zack?' Poppet asked as the Super Moshis hustled through the reception area of the Sandy Drain Hotel.

'I'm sure,' said Katsuma gruffly as he wrapped the Zoshling up in his cape.

'What about getting Missy Kix's autograph? She's my hero! I think I spot her over by the –'

'No time!' Katsuma growled.

Poppet sighed loudly.

'You-can-have-my-autograph-if-you-like-Poppet,' Rofl said shyly.

'Rofl really is a hero, Poppet,' said Luvli. 'He saved Zack from a hairy situation and us from being glooped.'

Poppet thought about it for a minute and slowly smiled.

'You're right! You really did save the day, Rofl,' she laughed. 'Come back with us to the *Rhapsody 2*. I'm sure Captain Squirk would love to thank you in person.'

The other Super Moshis all nodded in agreement and Rofl blushed even deeper.

'If-you-insist!' he chattered as they raced out of the gooperstar hotel.

Captain Squirk, Sprockett and Hubbs were waiting anxiously at the bottom of the *Rhapsody 2*'s ramp when the Super Moshis sped into the crash site.

'I could see on the ship's ZPS that you'd found a Zoshling,' said Squirk as he ran forward to meet them.

Katsuma carefully laid the weak Zoshling on the ground and drew back his cape.

Squirk inhaled sharply.

'It's First Officer Ooze!' he said. Squirk bent over his bewildered crewmate and ran a scanner across him. 'He's been drained of all his cosmic gloop!'

'What happened?' 'Where did you find him?'

'He was being held prisoner by an evil old cow at the Sandy Drain Hotel,' explained Poppet. 'She was testing it on Moshlings. It made Zack's hair grow!' Poppet blinked and clutched her chest.

'And she made hundreds of bottles of the stuff. She's up to no good, that's for sure,' said Katsuma.

'Unfortunately she activated a wrist device she was wearing and literally disappeared before we could find out anything more,' added Diavlo.

'What is this cosmic gloop, Captain Squirk?' asked Furi. 'It seems mighty dangerous.'

Squirk nodded sagely. 'Yes. It is a mysterious and very powerful substance. If it falls into the wrong hands, it could be disastrous.'

Diavlo turned to Sprockett and Hubbs.

'Does any of this sound familiar to you guys? Is this a C.L.O.N.C. thing?' he asked.

Sprockett and Hubbs stared sadly at the exhausted Ooze.

'Honestly, Diavlo, if we knew anything, we'd tell you,' said Hubbs.

Captain Squirk jumped to his feet and brushed the grass from his uniform.

'We'd better get Ooze on board the ship. Don't

worry, his cosmic gloop levels will soon be restored and he'll be perfectly all right.' He smiled reassuringly, then spotted Rofl chattering beside Furi.

'Why, hello!' Squirk said.

'This is Rofl, the Jabbering Jibberling,' said Zommer. 'He's the real hero of this rescue.'

'Stellar, Rofl!' Squirk cried excitedly. 'Sprockett and Hubbs will carry Ooze to sickbay and you can tell me exactly what happened.' He patted the little Moshling and looked up at the Super Moshis.

'And you can get going on the next part of your mission.'

'Huh?' said Zommer.

'I've found out where the *Rhapsody 2*'s chief medical officer, Dr. C. Fingz, is . . .'

'You picked up a reading on your ZPS?' Zommer asked.

'Not exactly!' Squirk chuckled. 'Somebody stuck this on the ship's window.'

He pulled out a poster from his pocket. It was

advertising a big circus, the Cirque du Bonbon, and various exciting acts including Zoshlingo, the amazing clairvoyant!'

Squirk jabbed a finger at the little purple creature. 'That isn't a clairvoyant,' he said. 'That is my crewmember.'

Poppet took the poster and studied it for a moment before rolling it up and stashing it in her backpack.

'We're on our way, Captain Squirk,' she smiled.

'Thank you, Super Moshis,' said the Captain gratefully. 'Oh. I do have one more favour to ask. Could you please pick up some space sandwiches on your way back? There appears to be a sandwich thief onboard the *Rhapsody 2* because lots of food is going missing!'

The Super Moshis turned to stare accusingly at Sprockett and Hubbs.

'Nuh-uh, it isn't us!' Hubbs said.

And, for once, he was telling the truth!

Chapter 5

CIRQUE du BONBON

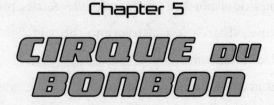

'I love the circus!' Zommer giggled excitedly as the Super Moshis spied the Cirque du Bonbon big top up ahead. 'The clowns and the strongman! The games and the stalls along Sideshow Smelly!'

'I like the candyfloss best,' said Furi, licking his lips greedily.

'Really? I like it every day of the week,' said Zommer.

'What?' Furi looked at Zommer, confused.

'Didn't you just say you liked Monday-floss?' Zommer asked. 'Because I like Monday, Tuesday and

Wednesday-floss! And all the other days of the week-floss as well!'

'I said candyfloss,' Furi said slowly. 'The sticky, pink stuff you eat?'

'Mmmm, Sunday-floss!' Zommer rubbed his belly happily.

Furi shook his head.

'OK, you know what, guys? Hush now,' said Poppet, scratching her head. 'We have to discuss our plan to rescue Dr. C. Fingz . . . or "Zoshlingo" as he's known here at the circus.'

'How about we just buy tickets to the show, Poppet,' said Diavlo. 'After his act we can talk to him about the *Rhapsody 2* and its mission to investigate

that mysterious growing star. Perhaps he's got a . . . percussion . . . discussion . . . oh, whatever you call it, and forgot who he is.'

'I think you mean "concussion",' Katsuma smiled. 'But, whatever, it's a good plan, Diavlo.'

The Super Moshis all nodded in agreement and joined the long queue of monsters waiting to get into the circus.

'Is that a Glump?' Furi asked, examining the small, scowling, squidgy ticket collector in clown make-up outside the tent. 'Let's have a look at that poster Captain Squirk found again, Poppet.'

Poppet rummaged around in her bag and pulled it out.

'There's Zoshlingo – the little purple dude with the squiggle on his head,' she said, pointing at his picture. 'And here's Pocito, with the lightning flash above his eyes,' said Katsuma, pointing at a little guy wearing a wrestling mask.

'And there's the Glump!' said Furi triumphantly, pointing at the image of the little grumpy clown.

'Except it says here it's called a "Clump",' Diavlo corrected him.

'Hmmmm. It does sound similar . . .' said Poppet.

And it looks exactly like a Glump – except it's wearing clown make-up!' Furi insisted.

'It certainly is a bit weird,' agreed Katsuma. 'That ringmaster, Candy the Clown, looks kind of familiar too.'

'We'll have to keep our eyes out for any funny business in there,' said Zommer.

'Well, "eye" in your case,' said Furi, pointing at the gaping socket where his left eye should have been.

The Super Moshis all laughed.

'OK. Let's get on with it,' said Katsuma, marching up to the Clump at the ticket booth.

'Five tickets to the show, please!' he said.

The Clump laughed for a moment, then barked, 'Sold out. NEXT!' and tried to brush the Moshis out of the way.

'Oh, but we really should have tickets waiting for us,' fibbed Poppet. 'Because we're friends of Zoshlingo and . . . er . . . well, he's expecting us.'

'Too bad!' said the nasty Clump. 'You should have bought tickets earlier. 'NEXT!'

'How rude!' Luvli huffed angrily. 'Leave this to me, Super Moshis.' And suddenly a Shimmering Sparkle Shower enveloped the bad-mannered Clump.

'We'd like tickets to the Big Top, please?' Luvli asked sweetly.

The Clump coughed and swatted at the glittery air.

'I hear Pocito the Mini Mangler – Cirque du Bonbon's resident strong-Moshling – might have some spare tickets,' it spluttered. 'Perhaps you could ask him.'

'That sounds wonderful,' smiled Luvli, batting her eyelashes. 'And where might we find Pocito?'

The Clump's eyes narrowed craftily in its blobby face.

'He's probably backstage warming up for his act,' it snickered. 'You know, backstage, where nobodies like you are forbidden to go? HAHAHA! See ya!'

The grumpy Clump yanked down the blind of his booth.

'I guess we should try our luck getting backstage,' Poppet said as the Supers wandered away. 'It's our only chance to find Zoshlingo.'

When the Super Moshis finally found the backstage area, they discovered to their dismay that it was guarded by another mean-looking Clump!

'Urgh! I like the look of that boof-head even less

than the first one,' said Luvli with a shudder. 'Still, let me go and ask politely – you never know!'

Luvli floated up to the growling Clump. 'Um, excuse me, do you think I could just ever so quickly pop backstage? My friend is waiting for me there.' She fluttered her eyelashes and smiled her most beguiling smile.

The Clump's frown didn't budge.

'D'you think I was born yesterday? Get lost,' he grumped, and turned his back on them.

The Super Moshis retreated a few steps and formed a huddle.

'What now?' asked Diavlo. 'If Luvli can't swing a backstage pass, no one can.'

'Wait! Shush, let me think!' Katsuma snapped, gripping his head in his hands in concentration. The other Moshis bit their lips and looked at the floor.

'I've got it!' he cried after a few moments. 'We need to create a diversion to get that Clump bozo away from the backstage area so we can get in there to talk to Pocito!'

'Nice idea!' said Zommer.

'If we're going to get that Clump's attention we'll need to create this diversion nearby,' said Luvli, gazing around. 'Sideshow Smelly is over there. Let's check it out and see what havoc we can cause.'

Zommer and Furi immediately started pumping their fists in the air.

'HAVOC! HAVOC! HAVOC!'

'Dudes, shhhhhhh! A diversion works better if the one you're trying to trick isn't expecting it, yeah?' explained Katsuma slowly.

'Oh . . . yeah . . . riiiight,' giggled Zommer.

Even so, as the Supers set off in the direction of Sideshow Smelly, Furi and Zommer were still furiously whispering, 'havoc, havoc, havoc'.

'Let's sabotage this game,' suggested Poppet as the Supers strolled past the Quack Attack stall on Sideshow Smelly. 'It's right opposite backstage and that Clump will have to come over and investigate.'

'How do we do that?' asked Luvli.

'Like this!' Zommer cried as he kicked the electrical plug out of its socket. The stall's tinny music and flashing lights shut down abruptly.

'Everybody be quiet and listen for the Clump,' whispered Katsuma.

Sure enough, they soon heard the mumbly grumblings of the Clump approaching.

'Stupid, stupid thing, always breaking down,' muttered the Clump. 'Now, where's that plug?'

Just as the Clump walked round the back of the stall to fix it, the Super Moshis slipped away unnoticed and darted over to the unguarded backstage area.

'Quick! Inside, Supers – let's find Pocito,' said Poppet, looking back to check the Clump wasn't coming.

Chapter 6

THE FAMOUS MINI MANGLER

The backstage area was almost as colourful as the tent itself! Around the perimeter of the enormous Big Top were brightly painted caravans where the circus performers cooked and slept. Half-open crates and trunks with costumes and magic apparatus spilling out of them took up every available space. There were mats for the tumblers and hanging rings for the highwire acts to practise on. It was incredible!

'We should think about joining the circus, Zom,' said Furi as he gazed around in wonder.

'What would we do for an act?' Zommer asked.

Furi scratched his head and thought for a moment.

'Trapeze? Tight-rope walker?' he suggested.

'What? But you hate heights! Remember the time we went to the Moshi Fun Park and you got giddy at the top of the Fear-Is Wheel?' Zommer scoffed.

Furi's stomach flipped over as he remembered how frightened he'd been.

'Urgh! Yeah . . .' he said.

'And remember the roller-ghoster ride? Half rollercoaster, half haunted house? You almost died of fright!' Zommer went on gleefully.

'Yeah, yeah, I remember! Forget I said anything,' huffed Furi, turning back to the others. 'Where is this Pocito, then?' he asked, following their gaze. A metre away from the Moshis stood a tiny masked Moshling pumping weights.

'*Dios mio*! Is it an autograph from the Fun Fair Champion of Strength you want, *amigos*?' the Moshling asked. 'You are forbidden from coming backstage, but I understand that the lure of meeting the famous Mini Mangler Pocito might prove too strong to resist!'

'Ye-es, that's it, Pocito,' said Katsuma. 'An autograph and any spare tickets you might have for the Big Top show?'

'First things first. A pen . . .' Pocito transferred the barbell he was holding to one hand and held out the other impatiently. Poppet scrabbled for a pen and

handed it to him, along with the Cirque du Bon Bon poster. Pocito scrawled his autograph across his picture and handed it back. 'And, now, about these spare tickets,' he said, dropping the barbell on the sawdust and flexing his muscles. 'As you know I am the major attraction of the circus. My feats of strength and derring-do are known throughout the world of Moshi! I am regularly shot out of cannons! Who else but Pocito, the Mini Mangler, could do this day after day? Eh? I ask you!'

The Super Moshis waited politely for Pocito to continue.

'No, really, I ask you the question! Who else?' Pocito pointed at Poppet.

'Um . . . nobody else . . . ?' Poppet hesitantly replied.

'¡*Si*! Now we are getting somewhere!' The Mini Mangler dropped to the floor and began doing one-armed push-ups. 'To get these tickets you want so badly, you will need to provide me with a Cherry Bomb plushie . . . each.'

'Uh . . . OK. That shouldn't be a problem.' Diavlo replied, relieved Pocito's needs weren't unreasonable. He'd heard of performing artists (like Blingo) demanding thirty plates of barfmallows with the green ones removed!

'The Cherry Bomb plushie is the second-best thing about the circus, after me!' Pocito continued, jumping up from the ground and striking poses in front of the Supers. 'So strong! So red! So explosive!'

'OK Pocito,' said Katsuma. 'Consider it done.'

'Hey,' Furi said suddenly, excitedly pointing to the ground next to one of the caravans. It was covered in paintings of candy canes and lollipops. 'A sandwich!'

Furi walked over, picked up the large blue sandwich and was just about to take a big bite when Poppet grabbed it out of his hand.

'Hey! I'm pretty sure that's one of Captain Squirk's missing space sandwiches!' she said, examining it, then peering round the back of the caravan.

'I wonder who dropped it – and what they're doing here,' mused Diavlo, peeking over her shoulder.

'Ahem! *Amigos* . . .' tutted Pocito behind them, tapping his foot impatiently. 'The show starts in ten minutes and the Mini Mangler waits for no Moshi.'

Poppet shoved the sandwich into her bag and the Moshis stood to attention.

'Yes, sorry, Pocito,' said Katsuma, leading them to the exit. 'We're on the case!'

Unfortunately, as soon as the Supers had found the Cherry Bomb plushie stall they came up against a major problem. They needed special tokens to pay for the plushies – and the Supers didn't have any!

'Play some games on Sideshow Smelly and earn the tokens,' the Clump stallholder sneered. 'Gah! It's not rocket science!'

'Y'know, these Clumps' attitudes are really getting me down,' Furi moaned as the Supers made their way to Sideshow Smelly.

Despite their many skills – super-strength, martial

arts, boogying, flying – the Supers barely won enough tokens to buy a Cherry Bomb plushie each. All the games on Sideshow Smelly had been rigged by the Clumps to make it harder for customers to earn tokens!

'Let's try that one over there,' suggested Diavlo, pointing to the Quack Attack game they'd unplugged earlier. It had toy guns that fired rubber-tipped arrows at moving cut-outs of DJ Quack – and, according to the score board, there was one special target – Burnie the Fiery Frazzledragon, who earned you a whopping hundred points! That meant serious tokens.

'Yuck! Shooting poor defenceless Moshlings is mean!' Poppet cried in disgust.

'They're only cardboard, Poppet,' said Diavlo. 'They're not real.' He picked up a gun and began firing at the ducks.

'Look, there's Burnie, shoot!' shouted Zommer, grabbing the gun and taking aim.

'No, no, wait!' screamed Poppet, swatting it out of his hand just as he was about to unleash a rain of rubber-tipped arrows. 'That isn't cardboard – that's a real Moshling!

'My goodness, she's right!' Luvli cried, pointing at the helpless Moshling as it squirmed under its rope binding. Someone had replaced the Burnie cut-out with the real thing!

'Quack, shave him! I mean, QUICK, SAVE HIM!' Diavlo spluttered.

'Wait! We can't annoy the Clumps any more. We need to put something in his place,' said Katsuma.

Suddenly, Luvli pointed back to the plushie stall. Leaning up against the side was a red cardboard shape they hadn't noticed before.

'Look, there's the Burnie cut-out for sale over there,' she said, flying over. 'I'd like to buy that, please,' she said, handing over the few tokens she'd won to the grumpy Clump stallholder. He sighed and handed over the cut-out.

'Right. Let's unplug this baby again and rescue poor Burnie!' said Furi.

The Super Moshis pulled the plug on the game once more and when it had come to a stop they released Burnie and replaced him with his cardboard counterpart.

Once untied, the exhausted Moshling sank to the ground behind the stall. He was covered all over in red circles where the rubber-tipped arrows had found their target.

'Don't worry, Burnie, you're safe now,' Luvli reassured the Moshling. 'And we'll show those Clumps a thing or two before the day's out!'

'You know what?' fumed Poppet angrily. 'First those Clumps – which I think *are* Glumps, like Furi said – then these terrible games you can never win at and now making a poor defenceless Moshling part of a horrible game? Cirque du BonBon stinks of C.L.O.N.C.!'

'You think?' Luvli said, worried. 'If Zoshlingo has fallen into C.L.O.N.C.'s hands, he might be in more danger than we'd imagined!'

'You're right,' Katsuma said gravely. 'We'd better sort out this Big Top ticket situation, pronto.'

'Yep. And now I can get us some major tokens,' said Zommer, plugging the game in again, picking up the gun and blitzing the Burnie cut-out as it rolled into view. The Super Moshis cheered as he picked up a hundred tokens.

The monsters hurried back to the stall and swapped their booty for a Cherry Bomb plushie each, much to the dissatisfaction of the Clump who served them. As Zommer took the paper bag, he felt something moving inside and peeped in warily. One of the plushies was alive!

'Hey, that isn't a plushie!' Zommer exclaimed. 'It's Cherry Bomb for real! With a fuse and everything!'

'Get that Moshling out of the paper bag – hurry! We don't want Cherry Bomb accidentally setting fire to the plushies!' Katsuma said and Zommer quickly

emptied the bag on to the ground. 'Whew! Cheers *fire* saving me, Super Moshis!' Cherry Bomb grinned, getting up off the ground. 'I know my way around the circus, so if *fuse* need my help, come and *fire-nd* me!'

And, with that, the little red Moshling disappeared into the crowd.

'Ahhh, you return bearing gifts!'

Pocito looked up from his exercises as the Supers slipped backstage, having unplugged the DJ Quack game for a second time. Clumps were pretty stupid, it seemed.

'We've got the plushies, Pocito –' Poppet began to say before the Mini Mangler cut her off.

'One . . . each?' he asked cautiously.

'Yes, one each,' sighed Poppet.

Pocito smiled, and with a flourish pulled a fistful of tickets from his stretchy uniform.

'Then here are your tickets!' he exclaimed as he grabbed the plushies from Zommer's grasp. 'I promise you will love the show just as much as I love my Cherry Bomb plushies.'

The Super Moshis looked at each other doubtfully – that didn't seem possible!

With the exchange made, Pocito turned to the Supers.

'Now we must *vamos*! I have a show to do!' he cried, waving the Supers out of the tent and pulling the flap closed behind them.

As the Moshis retreated, a door in one of the caravans creaked slowly open, out of sight. A massive tooth and a huge red nose appeared. It was Candy the Clown, Cirque du Bonbon's ringmaster! Silently, the gaudy figure sneaked round to the side of the caravan, flipped a lever and activated a communication device. A picture came fuzzily into view. It was the galley of a spaceship, with a chair turned away from the camera. All Candy the Clown could see was the gloved hand of the figure sitting in it, slowly stroking the arm of the chair.

'Agent ST reporting!' Candy Clown said.

'Go on, then. Report!' shouted a crackly voice.

'The Zoshling mind-reading plan is working,' giggled Candy the Clown. 'Moshi volunteers from the audience are allowing the Great Zoshlingo to read their minds. We now know exactly how many Moshlings each volunteer has – and where to find them!'

The voice made an ugly cackling sound and the gloved hand balled into a fist.

'Making it easier for me to capture Moshlings and turn them into Glumps!' the voice cried. 'Soon every Moshling will be glumped to build an unstoppable army to take over the Moshi world!'

The cackling grew louder and crazier, and Candy the Clown nodded excitedly.

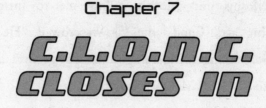

Chapter 7
C.L.O.N.C. CLOSES IN

Unaware of what was happening just outside the tent, the Super Moshis took their seats in the Big Top to watch the show.

A loud, crazy waltz was blaring out of the speakers, coloured flashing lights played across the sawdust ring and monsters from all over Monstro City chattered and laughed excitedly, waiting for the action to begin. The Super Moshis were rather enjoying themselves until the lights dimmed and came up again to reveal Candy the Clown standing in the middle of the ring.

'Time to pay attention,' hissed Katsuma.

'Moshis and Moshis! Allow me to introduce the big act!' Candy the Clown crowed. 'He's the strooooooongest Moshling in the woooooorld . . . it's Pocito the Mini Manglerrrrrrrrrrrr!'

The audience burst into applause as Pocito strutted into the ring and started flexing his muscles for the audience.

'I know we've talked about this before, but that ringmaster really reminds me of someone . . . or

something,' Luvli whispered.

Luvli studied Candy, noting the huge front tooth and the pink cottonwool hair.

'You're right, Luvli,' Poppet hissed excitedly. 'I think it's Sweet Tooth in disguise! My hunch was right. C.L.O.N.C. is behind the Cirque du Bonbon!'

As the lights faded to black and a spotlight shone on Pocito, the star of the Big Top, the Super Moshis were busy whispering amongst themselves.

Twenty minutes later the pint-sized Pocito's act was winding up.

'And for my last feat of strength and derring-do I, Pocito, shall be shot out of a cannon!' the Mini Mangler announced to a huge round of applause. 'This trick is not a fake! It is a real cannon, a real flame and a real Moshling cannonball – ME!'

Furi and Zommer exchanged looks.

'Pocito is awesome!' Zommer whispered.

'Do not be alarmed, *amigos*!' Pocito shouted from

the ring as he crawled into the mouth of the cannon.
'Watch the target hanging from the centre of the Big
Top! ¡*OLE*!'

In the darkness, the spotlight suddenly lit up a large
bullseye in the centre of the ring. The Supers could hear
a match striking and the fiery hiss of a slow-burning
fuse then . . . BOOM!

The Mini Mangler was catapulted out of the cannon,
he sailed over the sawdust-strewn ring and hit the
bullseye smack in the middle!

The audience leapt to their feet, cheering and hooting with excitement. The Super Moshis were hollering the loudest – they couldn't believe their eyes!

Pocito jumped up and lightly dusted the sawdust from his suit before taking a deep bow.

'¡*Ti amo*! I love you!' he cried, blowing kisses to the audience.

After one last bow, Pocito strode out of the Big Top, the sounds of adoration still ringing in his ears.

There was an interval before the next act so the Super Moshis left the Big Top to grab some overpriced Slop Corn and discuss the Sweet Tooth situation away from the crowds.

'What are we going to do about that candy-loving creep?' Poppet said.

'We need to unmask the villain! Show the crowds that's not some harmless ringmaster named Candy the Clown, but instead an evil operative of C.L.O.N.C!' Katsuma replied.

'But how?' Furi asked, scratching his head.

At that very moment Pocito swaggered up to the Supers.

'Did you enjoy the show, *amigos*?' he asked, knowing full well what the reply would be.

'It was totally rad, Pocito!' Zommer cried enthusiastically.

'Why, *graçias*,' replied Pocito with false-modesty. 'I do what I can . . .'

'It's funny you should say that, Pocito, because

you could really help us out with something now,' began Poppet. 'We've just discovered that Candy the Clown is in fact a criminal who goes by the name of Sweet Tooth.'

Pocito's eyes widened in disbelief.

'Sweet Tooth is part of a dastardly organization called C.L.O.N.C. – Criminal League Of Naughty Critters – who are out to destroy Monstro City!' she continued.

'We don't know what Sweet Tooth is up to getting involved in the circus, but we need your help to unmask this so-called Candy and prove there's something evil at work here!' Luvli said.

Pocito slowly shook his little masked head.

'Stop, stop, stop! You keep saying "unmask" . . .' he said. 'Don't you realize we've all got something to hide, *amigos*. One must respect the mask, whether worn by a hero or a villain.'

'But you don't understand. Sweet Tooth is nothing but a candy-hoarding crook!' Katsuma cried. 'Who'll stop at nothing! That creep forced our friend Burnie to take part in the Quack Attack game against his will! Moshis were shooting at him with rubber-tipped darts. He's covered in red dots where the suction cups stuck to him! He looks like he's got Moshi pox.'

'I'm sorry, *amigos*,' replied Pocito decidedly. 'But exposing this Sweet Tooth you speak of is not my destiny. I must follow my one true path. The path to rippling biceps, rock-hard abs and the occasional cheesy bean burrito.'

'But, Pocito . . .' Poppet began.

'There is no "but", *amiga mia*,' Pocito frowned. 'I cannot help you break the sanctity of the mask! You are mask-wearers yourselves – why is it so hard for you to understand what I'm saying?'

Before the Super Moshis could say another word, the Mini Mangler swept round and stalked off. Just as fast as his little legs would carry him.

Chapter 8

HIGH STRIKER

'We need Pocito on our side.' Katsuma looked around at his friends. 'He's the only one who can get us access to the artistes' part of the Big Top.'

'And he knows what Sweet Tooth's movements are during the show,' added Poppet. 'That's going to be a big help if we're to unmask that buck-toothed baddie!'

'OK, let's think,' said Diavlo, smoke billowing from his crater-head. 'How can we get Pocito's respect? What does he like?'

'He likes dressing in a onesie,' replied Zommer. 'And he likes a mask.'

'Correction. He loves a mask!' Furi chimed in. 'And he likes posing about and flexing his muscles. And being strong.'

'Furi, that's it!' Katsuma yelled suddenly. 'He likes strength. And we know someone really strong, don't we?'

A cloud of doubt passed over Furi's face. He frowned as he tried to think whom Katsuma must be talking about.

'We do?' he asked.

'You, you big lummox!' Zommer laughed.

'Oh yeah! ME!' Furi snickered.

'I see where you're going with this, Katsuma,' smiled Poppet. 'If Furi performs his own feats of strength, we might have a chance of getting Pocito's respect . . . and help.'

'That's the idea,' agreed Katsuma. 'And I see just the thing we need over there . . .'

Katsuma pointed to the Sideshow Smelly game opposite Quack Attack called High Striker. Contestants had to use a hammer to smash a lever,

which sent a puck hurtling up a tall tower to ring a bell at the top. The harder the hammer strike, the higher up the tower the puck would go. The higher the puck went, the more points the contestant would score.

'Let me at it!' Furi cried, racing over to the game.

'Hey look at this!' Zommer pointed at the leader board propped up beside High Striker. 'Pocito holds the top ten high scores. No one can beat him!'

'Pfft! We'll see about that!' Furi boasted as he made a grab for the huge hammer that was leaning against the tower. Furi lifted the hammer high above his head and began to carve out a circle in the air with it.

'Ready? Set? Go!' Furi screamed as he smashed the hammer down on to the lever with all his might.

The hammer immediately buckled in two and let out a raspberry.

PWEEEEEEEEEEEEE!

'Huh?' Furi looked at the puck that lay motionless at the bottom of the tower.

The Super Moshis crowded around and studied the hammer with mounting confusion.

'The game's rigged! This is nothing but a dodgy inflatable toy!' Diavlo exploded angrily as he prodded the hammer. 'No one could possibly ring the bell at the top tower with it!'

'Cheats! Rip off! BOO!' Zommer yelled furiously.

'Looks like we're going to have to cheat the cheaters, then,' Katsuma smiled craftily. 'As Pocito would say, "I have a plan, *amigos*".'

And the plan was this . . . simply add some much-needed weight to the hammer!

Where had the Super Moshis seen something heavy that would do the trick? One of the barbells Pocito had been using backstage would be perfect!

How would the Supers attach the barbell to the hammer? There was Clump gloop all over the ground wherever they looked.

'Right! Luvli? Diavlo? You fetch the barbell.' Katsuma ordered. 'Zom? Furi? Gather the goo! Everyone meet back here in ten.'

Luvli and Diavlo hovered outside the backstage area and exchanged looks. The Clump was stationed back in front of the entrance once again.

'How are we going to get Pocito's barbell with those two boof-heads standing guard?' Luvli muttered.

'How about I distract them while you fly in and grab it?' Diavlo suggested.

'Distract them how?' Luvli asked, but Diavlo was no longer there. He was already making a beeline for the bouncer.

'Yo, Pinky, what's up with that quiff?' Diavlo called as he swooped toward the Clump. 'What kind of product do you use to keep it so perky?'

The Clump in question was extremely fond of his pink quiff, and smirked proudly.

'Thanks for noticing,' he grinned toothily. 'I use a bit of Glump goo and –'

Aha! The Glump was out of the bag!

The Clumps are Glumps in clown make-up! Just like Poppet said! Diavlo thought to himself.

At that very moment Diavlo caught sight of Luvli darting out from backstage. The weight of the barbell she was carrying caused her to swerve erratically and she just missed bashing the Glump on the head with it!

Diavlo hovered awkwardly.

'Er, well . . . I better . . . um . . . fly . . . literally.' He snickered.

'Fine, buzz off!' the Glump sneered as he swatted at the Super Moshi.

And Diavlo did!

By the time Diavlo arrived back at the High Striker game the final part of the plan had been put into action. Furi had already attached the barbell to the hammer with Glump goo he and Zommer had collected.

'All ready, Katsuma.' Furi said. 'I'm going to smash that puck so hard it's going to fly out the top of the tower and right over the top of Mount Sillimanjaro!'

'Before you do that, Furi, there's something you guys need to know,' Diavlo said. 'It's –'

'Not now, Diavlo,' Poppet interrupted. 'It can wait. Furi has to get the high score!'

'But the Clumps are –' Diavlo tried again.

'Diavlo, later!' Zommer frowned.

Diavlo's head began to steam with frustration, but he kept quiet.

'OK, here goes.' Furi grunted, psyching himself up.

He strained to lift the hammer above his head and brought it down on the lever as hard as he could.

The puck immediately shot up the tower and rang the bell with a loud *BONG!*

'Yaaaay! Well done, Furi!' The Super Moshis cheered. Not only had Furi rung the bell, he'd also knocked Pocito off the top spot of the High Striker leader board!

'Furi! Furi! Furi!' Zommer chanted as he punched the air excitedly.

'What? What is this?' an astonished voice asked suddenly.

It was Pocito! The sound of the bell had summoned him to the High Striker game.

'My unbroken record in High Striker lies in tatters!' he cried as he gazed sadly at the leader board. 'Is it possible one of you puny Super Moshis is imbued with a hidden strength of which I'd previously been unaware?'

Pocito stopped, his eyes brimming with tears. He looked around in a confused fashion.

'*Dios mio*, what is this? Why do these Clumps circle us as if we were pieces of succulent fried chicken

straight from the pan with perhaps a little picante sauce on the side?'

For the ring of the High Striker bell had not only summoned Pocito, but also the Glumps who'd rigged it. And now they wanted to know who'd messed with their game!

'Uh, yeah, dudes? Like I've been trying to tell you for the last five minutes, the Clumps are Glumps dressed as circus clowns,' sighed Diavlo.

Chapter 9

MOSHLING MINDREADING

The Glumps quickly formed a ring round our hopelessly outnumbered heroes and began closing in.

'Er . . . we could've done with that bit of information just a little earlier, Diavlo,' said Poppet shaking her head.

'These Clumps, Glumps, whatevers – are going to get it!' Furi growled, his fur bristling with excitement.

'Ooooh! Look at the Abominable Snowman there with his fur all sticking up on end!' one of the Glumps sneered in return.

'Get ready, Super Moshis,' cried Katsuma. 'On my say so . . .'

The Supers and Pocito all assumed their fighting positions!

Katsuma put his arms up in a karate pose. Poppet raised her paws. Steam began to pour from Diavlo's lava head. Luvli's star-tipped stem whipped from side to side. Zommer started whirling his arms around randomly. Furi stood with his legs astride and Pocito flexed his mighty mini muscles.

The Glumps meanwhile had stopped in their tracks and begun to look nervous instead!

'SUPERS . . . STRIIIIIIIIIKE!' Katsuma hollered.

On this sign the Supers and Pocito rushed straight at the Glumps with fangs bared, glitter flying and capes a-fluttering.

The cowardly Glumps took one look at their brave opponents racing toward them and as one big blubbery mass they turned and bounded away!

'Retreat, Glumps . . . I mean, Chumps . . . I

mean CLUMPS!' they called to each other as they rolled under tents and caravans, inside sideshows and concession stands.

In no time at all the Glumps had completely disappeared and the Supers and Pocito found themselves alone.

The Mini Mangler turned to Katsuma, his eyebrows raised in surprise.

'You may look like a harmless woodland creature in a mask,' he said as he shook Katsuma by the paw. 'But you and your friends fight like musky huskies! I have much respect for the musky husky. It is lean, mean, keen and rarely seen. And you, *mis amigos*, are all of these things. Tell me how the Mini Mangler can serve you.'

'Thanks, Pocito,' Katsuma replied gratefully. 'We're on a rescue mission and our target is Dr. C. Fingz. He's working at the Cirque du Bonbon under the name Zoshlingo. We need to know from you when he's due to perform his act.'

'That is easy!' Pocito replied. 'He will perform in the Big Top at any moment. But you didn't need my help for this. What do you really need from Pocito?'

'Well, the whole plan is we grab the Zoshling and make sure he's safe. Then we unmask . . . er, I mean, *expose* Sweet Tooth,' said Furi, eyeing the Mini Mangler warily. 'The one you know as Candy the Clown.'

'OK,' said Pocito, nodding. 'I'll do it.'

The house lights in the Big Top dimmed as the Supers and Pocito took their seats. A spotlight suddenly lit the middle of the ring and Candy the Clown – AKA Sweet Tooth – appeared, grinning madly.

'Allow me to introduce our next act,' Sweet Tooth squeaked as the applause of the crowd died down. 'He may be small, but he's got a lot on his mind . . . including what's on your mind. HAHAHA! He's Zoshlingo – mindreader extraordinaaaaaaaaaaaaaaaire!'

The tiny purple Zoshling wandered into the ring to join Sweet Tooth. He looked as if he wasn't quite

sure where he was or what he was doing there!

'Poor thing,' murmured Luvli sadly. 'The sooner we get Dr. C. Fingz back to the *Rhapsody 2* the better.'

The Supers nodded.

'I need a volunteer from the audience! Step right this way!' said Sweet Tooth.

The Supers exchanged looks. Which of them would be the best candidate for mindreading?

Katsuma? No! Dr. C. Fingz might accidentally reveal the Supers' plan to rescue him in front of Sweet Tooth.

Zommer? With his sawdust-stuffed skull? Definitely not.

Diavlo? No. Too much of a hot-head! Literally.

Luvli? Poppet? Furi . . . ? FURI!!

'Why is it always me?' Furi moaned as all eyes turned on him.

'Just put your hand up,' Diavlo said, digging him in the ribs.

'Ahh, we have a volunteer!' Sweet Tooth announced,

catching sight of Furi's raised hand. 'Come forward!'

As he tripped down the stairs to enter the ring, Furi heard two little voices from the audience cheering him on.

'Go, Furi!' Burnie cried.

'You're famous!' Cherry Bomb giggled.

Furi gave them a little wave as he joined Dr. C. Fingz and Sweet Tooth in the ring.

'I will now proceed to read the mind of this Moshi volunteer and reveal to you all how many Moshlings he has!' Fingz announced.

The little Zoshling had a curly green antenna coming out of his head and it began to glow as he spoke.

Furi closed his eyes. He didn't really believe that Fingz would be able to read his mind, but something was happening in his head. It felt as if somebody were ferreting around his brain!

'You have . . . forty-two Moshlings!' Fingz said triumphantly.

The hushed crowd waited expectantly to see what Furi would say.

Furi opened his eyes and stared at Fingz in astonishment. He nodded his head slowly.

'Yes,' Furi whispered. 'I do have forty-two Moshlings.'

The audience immediately jumped to its feet and broke into thunderous applause! Using the noise of the crowd as cover, Furi quickly took the opportunity to talk to Fingz without Sweet Tooth overhearing.

'With your incredible mindreading skill, haven't you discovered yet that Candy the Clown is none other than Sweet Tooth, an evil psycho with a taste for sugar and a leading member of C.L.O.N.C?' he whispered.

'It's all been so confusing!' Fingz replied. 'My spaceship crashed and my circuits were addled. I couldn't locate my fellow Symphonians. Then Candy the Clown and the Cirque du Bonbon took me in. Later I began to receive random garbled messages. I-I-It's all too much . . .'

The little Zoshling clutched his head painfully.

'Well, don't worry any more. We're here to take you back to the *Rhapsody 2*,' said Furi reassuringly.

Now it was Dr. C. Fingz's turn to be amazed.

'You know about the *Rhapsody 2*? And Captain Squirk? And Ooze?' he asked hopefully.

'Yes, and me and my friends are going to get you out of this Cirque du Nightmare and back with them just as soon as possible,' Furi assured him.

Dr. C. Fingz smiled.

'Now, tell me about these messages you're receiving?' Furi asked.

'They're distress signals mainly,' said Fingz. 'They pop into my head at the most awkward moments. Something about someone called . . .' Fingz closed his eyes and concentrated. '. . . Furi . . . ?'

'Yes?' Furi asked, leaning forward.

'Yes, Furi,' said Fingz again.

'Yes, what?'

'That's the name my antenna is picking up. Furi.'

Furi's head was beginning to spin.

'OK . . . But. What's. The. Name?' Furi asked slowly.

'The. Name. Is. Furi,' Fingz replied extra slowly.

Furi shook his head, but there was no time for more explanation. The crowd were beginning to quieten down and Sweet Tooth was calling for another volunteer.

Chapter 10
AN EXPLOSIVE ENDING

Once his time in the spotlight was over, Furi was escorted from the ring by some clownish Glumps and pushed out of the Big Top.

He was standing there wondering what to do next when the Supers and Pocito suddenly appeared by his side.

'Nice job, Furi,' Diavlo said, patting his friend on the back. 'You were a natural up there!'

'Thanks, D, it was kind of scary standing in front of all those Moshis!' Furi said. 'But I saw Burnie and Cherry Bomb in the audience so I had to act cool, y'know!'

'So what did you find out from Fingz?' Poppet asked excitedly. 'Did he know that Candy was Sweet Tooth? Does he know why Sweet Tooth's pretending to be a ringmaster? Is Sweet Tooth hatching an evil plan?'

'Whoa, Poppet! One question at a time!' Furi said, holding up his hands to stop his friend's endless questions.

'Sorry, sorry. Just take your time.' Poppet giggled apologetically.

'Firstly, Fingz's' antenna has gone haywire since the *Rhapsody 2* crash-landed and he keeps picking up random distress signals,' explained Furi.

'From who?' Katsuma asked.

'He didn't say. He just talked in circles. He kept repeating my name all the time. I think his antenna is pretty fried!' Furi said.

'What if it wasn't your name Fingz was repeating, but the name of whoever was sending the distress signal?' Luvli suggested.

Diavlo's jaw fell open.

'What if it was a
signal from Elder Furi?'
he asked.

The Supers exchanged
shocked looks.

'Who is this Elder
Furi you speak of?'
Pocito piped up.

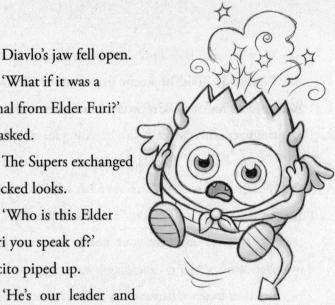

'He's our leader and
he's been missing since Sweet Tooth and the rest of the
corrupt C.L.O.N.C. crew tried to destroy Monstro
City!' Poppet explained.

'Then we should capture this Sweet Tooth and
make it squawk like a chicken!' Pocito declared. 'The
question is how?'

'I know!' Katsuma cried suddenly. 'With the
cannon! We can load the real Cherry Bomb into
Pocito's cannon, then ask Burnie to light his fuse. We
can blow Sweet Tooth right out of the ring!'

'Wow! Great idea!' Zommer said approvingly.

'Come on! There's no time to waste!' Diavlo cried.
'We need to round up Cherry and Burnie and put this
plan into action!'

When the Supers and Pocito re-entered the Big Top,
Dr. C. Fingz's act was just winding up.

'OK, Poppet and Zommer? You guys go get
Burnie and Cherry Bomb and fill them in on the
plan,' whispered Diavlo. 'The rest of us will preapre
the cannon.'

'We'll be as quick as we can,' said Poppet, grabbing
Zommer and heading into the audience.

'I will just take the cover off the front . . . like
so.' Pocito whipped off the material that lay over the
muzzle of the cannon. 'We will point it towards the
centre of the ring . . . like so.' He cranked a handle on
the side of the cannon and the weapon slowly swung
into position, pointing directly at Sweet Tooth.

'And . . . ¡*bueno*! . . . we are ready, *amigos*.'

The Supers nervously watched Fingz and Sweet Tooth take their final bows. The act was over, but where were Poppet and Zommer? They were running out of time!

'Sweet Tooth's signalling to the Glumps to bring up the house lights! They're going to clear the Big Top!' Luvli cried. 'We need Burnie and Cherry Bomb here now!'

'Did somebody say our names?' a little voice chimed in.

Poppet and Zommer were back in the nick of time and they had the two little Moshlings with them!

'Everything ready?' Poppet gasped, out of breath.

'Ready!' said Katsuma.

Cherry Bomb leapt off Zommer's shoulders straight into the firing chamber of the cannon.

'You OK in there, Cherry?' Furi asked with concern as the Moshling wiggled its way into position.

'Hee hee! It's a tight fit, but I'm gonna have a blast!' Cherry giggled.

'What about you, Burnie? Are you ready to light the fuse?' Zommer asked.

'I'm all fired up!' Burnie replied, a spurt of flame shooting out of its mouth.

'Then *vamonos*, *amigos*! Candy the Clown is directly in our sights!' Pocito cried as he crawled inside the cannon. 'Fire when ready!'

With a deafening bang the cannon roared into life and the brave Mini Mangler shot into the ring and bowled Sweet Tooth backwards to the ground!

A hush fell over the audience. What had happened? Was this cannon thing part of Zoshlingo's act? A Moshi in the crowd began to clap hesitantly. Then surrounding Moshis joined in. Pretty soon the crowd was on its feet cheering for more!

Meanwhile, Sweet Tooth lay on the ground, recovering. Stars danced around the villain's head and it became clear the dastardly game was up!

'You meddling Super Moshis haven't heard the last of me,' Sweet Tooth squeaked angrily as the Supers raced into the ring. 'C.L.O.N.C. will have its revenge!'

Pocito, who was flexing his muscles and greatly enjoying the extra applause, scoffed in Sweet Tooth's face.

'You're finished, Candy! The Supers may not know

your plans, but they soon will – once Zoshlingo has
read your poisonous mind!'

Sweet Tooth scowled furiously and began frantically
fiddling with a small wrist device.

'Sweet Tooth has the same wrist thingy as Frau
Now BrownKau –'

But Katsuma's warning came too late and Sweet
Tooth disappeared before their eyes.

The excited hoots and cheers of the audience grew

louder as the Supers hustled Fingz and their Moshling friends from the Big Top.

Dr. C. Fingz breathed a long sigh of relief.

'Thank you all for rescuing me from the clutches of that insane clown!' he cried. 'I had to find out how many Moshlings the citizens of Monstro City had . . . and then after the act, backstage, I had to locate where they all were! It was simply exhausting just looking for the same thing in the brains of all those volunteers . . . I was completely overwhelmed!'

Katsuma balled his paw into a fist. 'So that's what that candy creep is up to!'

'What? I don't get it,' said Zommer, scratching his head.

'Sweet Tooth is reading Moshis' minds to find out where all our Moshlings are! And what does C.L.O.N.C. love to do to Moshlings?' cried Katsuma.

'Steal them . . .' said Luvli, shivering.

'. . . and glump them,' said Poppet miserably.

'Oh,' said Zommer. 'What a horrible thought. And now the nasty criminal has disappeared.'

'But thanks to you Super Moshis – and you too little Moshlings,' he added, patting Burnie on the head, 'Sweet Tooth can't use me any more. I'm safe once again and ready to return to the *Rhapsody 2*.'

'You're right. We'll catch up with Sweet Tooth all in good time,' said Furi, narrowing his eyes.

'It'll take some time to reach the ship, Doctor,' said Poppet. 'It crash-landed on the other side of Music Island.'

Fingz grinned as his antenna began to sizzle.

'Heh heh, I don't think so,' he chuckled. 'I've already contacted Captain Squirk and he's organizing to have us transpor– Oh, here we go!'

Suddenly the Supers, the Zoshling and all three Moshlings were enveloped in a cloud of cosmic dust. When it finally cleared, they had all vanished.

When they rematerialized, the Super Moshis and
Moshlings found themselves standing in the clearing
beside the *Rhapsody 2*.

'Dr. C. Fingz!' Captain Squirk cried as he rushed
forward to hug his crewmate. 'First Officer
Ooze and I have been so worried!'

'And we were a bit worried about you, Supers,' Sprockett said shyly as he and Hubbs patted Zommer awkwardly on the back. 'Anyway, we're glad you're here.'

'Not least because I'm starving for a space sandwich!' cried Captain Squirk.

'Oh yes! The space sandwich!' Poppet cried, opening her backpack. 'I totally forgot about that!'

Captain Squirk's face lit up.

'You found one?' he asked.

The Super Moshis smiled.

'Yep – it looks kind of funky, but everyone has different taste, I guess!' laughed Poppet, handing the blue sandwich to the Zoshling captain.

Squirk grinned and took a big bite. 'Thank you, Super Moshis – you're the best,' he said, spluttering space crumbs everywhere. 'So, did you figure out who was behind all this?'

'Yes!' said Diavlo. 'It was that sugary menace, Sweet Tooth – disguised as the circus ringmaster.'

'Sweet Tooth was stealing my space sandwiches?' said Squirk, horrified.

'Er, no . . .' said Furi. 'Sweet Tooth was using Dr. C. Fingz to read the monsters' minds!'

'Why would Sweet Tooth want to do that?' said Squirk, shoving the last of the sandwich into his little mouth.

'To find out how many moshlings each monster has . . . so C.L.O.N.C. could steal them!' cried Poppet.

'But . . . what in the Swooniverse is C.L.O.N.C.?' asked the captain.

Katsuma crossed his arms. 'They're a league of

criminals that were trying to destroy Monstro City . . . and it looks like they're back.'

'Holy space blasters!' exclaimed Captain Squirk. 'Thank the stars you were there – and for saving Fingz!'

Katsuma smiled.

'Well. We'll have to get to the bottom of this C.L.O.N.C. conundrum but rescuing Dr. Fingz isn't bad for a day's work.'

He looked at the Super Moshis standing beside him, who beamed with pride too.

'Oh, and we also managed to bring back Pocito the Mini Mangler!' Zommer cried. 'And Cherry Bomb and Burnie the Fiery Frazzledragon!'

'Welcome aboard!' Captain Squirk grinned happily.

Later that night, after the Moshis and Moshlings had gone back to their beds in Mostro City for a much-needed sleep, the Zoshlings stepped out of the *Rhapsody 2* to study the night sky.

'The mysterious star our Symphonian scientists sent us to investigate grows bigger by the day,' said Squirk, wringing his hands.

'Yes, and it's having a disastrous effect on the Moshis' world,' Ooze agreed. 'I've run tests and they confirm our worst fears. The bigger the star grows, the faster the snow melts on Mount Sillimanjaro.'

'But the rising snow melt runs downhill directly into the sea! Monstro City could be underwater in a matter of weeks!' Fingz exclaimed.

'Which is why we must locate our final crewmember, Splutnik, and the ship's missing steering wheel,' said Squirk. 'Then and only then can we continue our mission. The ZPS will be running thirty-two/seven until we find them.'

'We need to hurry,' said Ooze, looking up into the night sky. 'So we can send the Super Moshis on their next mission and save Monstro City.'

Meanwhile, onboard the *Rhapsody 2*, Sprockett and Hubbs were getting ready to power down for the night.

'Night, Hubbs,' said Sprockett sleepily.

'Night, Spr– Hey, did you hear that?' Hubbs murmured, already half asleep.

'What?'

'I thought I heard someone whisper "the doctor will see you now" . . .' Hubbs said, his electronic eyelids drooping.

'It was just a dream . . . Hu . . . zzzzzzzz . . . zzzz . . .'
Sprockett said, falling asleep.

Or was it?

The action continues in Music Island Missions: Masters
of the Swooniverse!

Don't miss the next exciting Music Island Mission
adventure, coming soon in paperback and ebook:

Read an exclusive extract on the next page!

Chapter 1

THE GHOSTLY GOOEY GALLEON

First Officer Ooze checked the *Rhapsody 2*'s ZPS readings.

'Great gloops! I've found something Captain,' he called.

'You've located Chief Engineer Splutnik, the last of our missing crewmembers?' the captain asked hopefully as he crossed the spaceship's bridge to join Ooze at the controls.

'Not yet, Captain,' said Ooze. 'But the ZPS has located a replacement steering device for the one that was damaged when we crash-landed here on Music Island.'

'Well, that's a start,' replied the Captain. 'But it's useless if we can't find Splutnik! We need the entire crew aboard to power the ship and continue our mission to investigate that mysterious growing star.'

'That star continues to have a disastrous effect on the Moshi world,' added Dr. C. Fingz, the *Rhapsody 2*'s chief medical officer. 'The closer it gets, the faster the snow on Mount Sillimanjaro melts and the higher the water levels rise. We must investigate before Monstro City finds itself underwater! Where's this steering device located, Ooze?'

Ooze checked his coordinates.

'It's in the ocean, east of Music Island,' he said. 'Onboard some kind of ancient floaty thing made of wood.'

'I'll summon the Super Moshis,' said Squirk.

'It's a ship,' said Zommer as the Super Moshis' dinghy neared its destination.

'No, it's a pirate ship! Look, the name's written on the side,' exclaimed Diavlo.

'The *Gooey Galleon*,' said Luvli, reading the writing.

'Oh, terrific. Pirates,' moaned Furi.

They pulled in alongside the pirate ship.

'Ahoy, matey dudes!' Zommer called up. 'Throw us down ye rope ladder. We want to come aboard!'

'Ahoy? Ye?' Poppet giggled. 'What are you talking about, Zom?'

'I'm speaking Olde Piratey,' said Zommer. 'They won't understand us otherwise.'

'Yeah, well, I'm not sure that real pirates talk that way. It's only in storyboo—'

A face suddenly appeared over the side of the *Gooey Galleon*.

'Aaaaaarrrrr! Ahoy to ye all!' it hollered, flinging down a rope ladder. 'Come aboard, me hearties.'

Poppet's eyes widened.

'Wow. Guess I was wrong,' she laughed.

The Super Moshis stood in silence on the deck of the ship and tried not to gawk at the pirate standing before them. It was strange. He wore a white sailor's cap and an eye patch. He lived on a galleon. He had a toothy grin and said 'aaaaarrrr'. In almost every respect he was exactly as a pirate should be. Except the Super Moshis could see straight through him.

'Arrrr see ye never met a ghost pirate a'fore,' he chuckled. 'Jaunty Jack be me name. Arrrr'm first mate of the *Gooey Galleon*. What can we be doin' for ye, me hearties?'

'We're the Super Moshis and we've come to ask you a big favour,' said Poppet, smiling sweetly.

'What be this favourrrrrr?' Jaunty Jack asked.

Poppet nodded towards the large wooden steering wheel in the middle of the deck.

'Our friends' ship crashed and its steering wheel broke. We were wondering if we could possibly have yours . . .?' she asked hopefully.

'Aaaarrrr sympathize with ye friends' situation,'

Jaunty Jack said, his eyes misting over. 'We be havin'
some problems of aaaarrrr own. Ever since we nabbed
aaaarrrselves some booty from Hong Bong Island we be
in the grip of a beastly curse.'

'What happened?' Poppet asked.

'We were the most feared pirates of the Seventy
Seas until that fateful journey to Hong Bong,' said
Jaunty Jack gravely. 'We had it all! We dined off
golden platters. We ate with silver spoons. We slept on
mattresses stuffed with Rox . . .'

'That sounds uncomfortable, dude,' Zommer
whispered to Diavlo.

'. . . but it all changed after that accursed kitty came
aboard,' Jaunty Jack continued. 'Since then the *Gooey
Galleon* be marooned on this sandbank and we be goin'
nowhere . . .'

'Great! So you won't need that steering wheel, then,'
said Furi happily.

The Super Moshis all frowned at Furi.

'Whaaaaaat? What did I say?' Furi asked, confused.

Katsuma rolled his eyes and turned back to Jack. 'You have a cat problem?' he asked.

'Tingaling, the Kitten of Good Fortune, they call her,' Jack said with a sigh. 'She be part of the Hong Bong Island booty, but she ain't brought us nothin' but misery.'

He hung his ghostly head mournfully.

'That's a real shame, Jack,' said Furi, shaking his head. 'But you really won't be needing that steering wheel, then, will you?'

Jaunty Jack looked up and his face suddenly broke into a smile.

'Har har! Ye be right, matey. Ye can have it and good luck to ye!'

While Katsuma and Poppet busied themselves undoing the bolts that held the ship's steering wheel in place, the rest of the Supers chatted to Jaunty Jack.

'It's very quiet onboard the *Gooey Galleon*,' said

Diavlo. 'Where's the rest of the crew?'

'We be havin' a big belchin' contest this aaaaarrrrfternoon, so Captain Codswallop and the rest of the crew be preparin',' explained Jack.

'Ahoy!' someone cried from the crow's nest high above the deck. The Supers looked up in surprise.

'Speakin' of one of the rascally devils . . .' chuckled Jack. 'Here be McDuff. Hold on to ye masks, Super Moshis, he's been acting mighty strange since that cat came aboard!'

McDuff suddenly grabbed a rope and slid down it towards Katsuma and Poppet.

'WHEEEEEEEEEE!' he cried, his red spotted bandana fluttering in his wake.

'What in marine madness is this?' Katsuma yelled as McDuff bared his teeth and grabbed the steering wheel from his paws.

'Come back with that!' Poppet cried, trying to swipe it back.

But McDuff was too quick. He shot up out of

reach and flung the steering wheel into the sea!

Everyone rushed to the side of the ship and watched in horror as it disappeared beneath the waves.

'Aaaaarrrrr,' said Jaunty Jack, frowning. 'That'll go right to the bottom of the Potion Ocean and it's verrrrrry deep. Looks like you'll be needin' our divin' suit, me Supers . . . if ye can find it.'

'What do you mean *if*?' asked Luvli, but Jack didn't have a chance to answer.

'By the powers of King Neptune and aaarrrrll his fishy friends, where aaarrrrr you, Jack?' screamed a voice from the captain's cabin.

Jaunty Jack immediately snapped to attention.

'That's Captain Codswallop! Aaarrr better go!' he said, floating off speedily and disappearing through the wall.

Poppet sighed. 'So that means we've got to find this diving suit, fetch the steering wheel from the bottom of the sea and . . . Furi, would you please stop making that silly noise and pay attention?'

'It's not me, Poppet,' said Furi. 'I thought it was Diavlo.'

'Me?' Diavlo huffed. 'Don't be a furry fool!'

Luvli cleared her throat. 'It's not any of us,' she said. 'The noise is coming from over there.' Luvli pointed at the carved green figurehead at the prow of the ship. Its head was trapped in a diving helmet, and it was squealing for help.